GYMNASTICS

How to Play the All-Star Way

By **Dwight Normile**

Introduction by **Tatiana Gutsu**

Illustrated by **Dwight Normile**

Photographs by **Eileen Langsley** and **Mary Pat Boron**

★ An **Arvid Knudsen** book ★

**RAINTREE
STECK-VAUGHN**
P U B L I S H E R S
The Steck-Vaughn Company

Austin, Texas

Dedication

With thanks to my sister, Candi, who introduced me to
the sport of gymnastics when I was 9 years old.
And to my wife, Pam for her unconditional support.

Acknowledgments

Photographs from the collection of Eileen Langsley, pp. 4, 5, 9, 14,
26, 30, 34, and 38.
Photographs from the collection of Mary Pat Boron, cover and pp. 6, 10,
18, 25, 42, and 45.
Electronic composition by DAK Graphics

© Copyright 1996, Steck-Vaughn Company

Published by Raintree Steck-Vaughn Publishers, an imprint of
Steck-Vaughn Company.

Library of Congress Cataloging-in-Publication Data

Normile, Dwight.
Gymnastics/by Dwight Normile; introduction by Tatiana Gutsu;
illustrations by Dwight Normile;
photographs by Eileen Langsley and Mary Pat Boron.
p. cm. — (How to play the all-star way)
"An Arvid Knudsen Book."
Includes bibliographical references and index.
Summary: Describes the techniques of various events of this very old sport
and refers to contemporary gymnasts who excel in each activity.
ISBN 0-8114-6595-0 (hardcover)
1. Gymnastics—Juvenile literature. [1. Gymnastics.]
I. Langsley, Eileen, ill. II. Boron, Mary Pat, ill. III. Title. IV. Series.
GV461.N57 1996
796.44—dc20   95-44188   CIP   AC
Printed and bound in the United States

1 2 3 4 5 6 7 8 9 0   99 98 97 96 95

CONTENTS

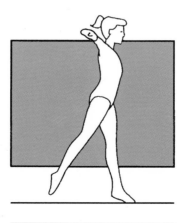

Tatiana Gutsu

INTRODUCTION

When I was six years old, my parents took me to a local gymnastics club. The coaches asked me to do a few exercises to see if I had any potential. They must have liked what they saw, because I was invited to join the team. Like most young gymnasts, my dream was to become the Olympic champion. In 1992 my dream came true in Barcelona, Spain.

We often hear that a child must sacrifice too much to be a world-class gymnast. I never felt that way. Gymnastics was so much fun that I didn't mind all the hard work. I really feel lucky to have been involved in gymnastics. I got to travel all over the world, experience different cultures, and meet new friends.

Now I am 18 and still training. I stay in shape to perform in exhibitions. Gymnastics has been my life for many years, and I love it.

Dwight Normile's book, *Gymnastics: How to Play the All-Star Way*, will help you understand more about gymnastics. Gymnastics is an activity that develops strength, flexibility, and coordination. It also teaches self-discipline and teamwork.

Remember, to be successful in anything, you must work very hard. It helps if you enjoy what you are doing. I believe you will have fun with gymnastics. Who knows? Maybe you, too, will become an Olympic champion. Good luck to everyone.

—*Tatiana Gutsu (Ukraine),*
1992 Olympic all-around champion

◀ Tatiana Gutsu (Ukraine), 1992 Olympic all-around champion. She was a member of the Commonwealth of Independent States team (former Soviet Union).

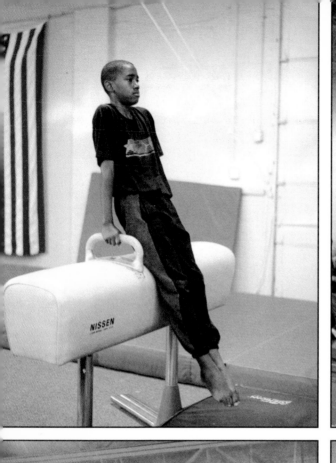

ABOUT GYMNASTICS

Gymnastics is a very old sport. Through the years, it has gone through many changes. The ancient Greeks were the first to do gymnastics. It was a form of physical exercise for them, and they wore no clothes! The word *gymnastics* comes from the Greek word *gymnos*, which means naked.

The modern form of gymnastics began in the 1700s in Germany. Friedrich Ludwig Jahn is called the "Father of Gymnastics." His Turn Vereins, or gymnastics clubs, spread throughout Germany in the early 1800s. In 1848, the first American Turners, modeled after the Turn Vereins, opened in Cincinnati, Ohio.

Other gymnastics groups surfaced in the United States later. The Czechoslovakian Sokols, for example, organized a club in St. Louis in 1865. In 1869 the YMCA built gymnastics facilities in San Francisco and New York.

In 1885 the Amateur Athletic Union (AAU) was formed. The AAU was the official governing body for American gymnastics for many years. In 1963 the U.S. Gymnastics Federation (USGF) was founded. The USGF is now called USA Gymnastics.

Although the ancient Greeks did gymnastics for exercise, today's gymnasts participate in competitions. The ultimate goal of most gymnasts is to compete in the Olympics.

◀ (upper left) Pommel horse exercise
(upper right) V hold exercise on balance beam
(lower left) Pike position
(lower right) All gymnasts must learn tumbling.

Gymnastics was a part of the first modern Olympics in Athens, Greece, in 1896. The competition was held outdoors, and only men competed. In 1928 women's competition was added. The competitive events have changed since then, and the gymnastics equipment has become more modern. Today, gymnastics is one of the most popular Olympic sports.

HOW GYMNASTS ARE SCORED BY JUDGES

The highest score a gymnast can achieve for each routine is 10.0.
In the Olympics, judges in women's gymnastics look for the following:
3.00: Value Parts (each skill is rated by how difficult it is)
0.60: Bonus Points (awarded for difficult skills)
2.00: Combination (routine construction)
4.40: Execution (how the routine is performed)
Judges in men's gymnastics look for the following:
2.40: Difficulty (each skill is rated by how difficult it is)
5.40: Exercise Presentation (how the routine is performed)
1.20: Special Requirements (different for each apparatus)
1.00: Bonus Points (awarded for difficult skills)
You shouldn't worry about your scores. You really have no control over them anyway. Says 1991 world champion Kim Zmeskal, "I love to compete. I don't really have anything to say about who's going to win and who's going to get each score, so I just do my job."

How to Get Started in Gymnastics

If you want to become a gymnast, there are gymnastics clubs in every state. The United States has more than 3,000 gymnastics clubs. Most of them are listed in the phone book. You can also enroll in a gymnastics class at your local YMCA.

As a beginner, you will probably take a one-hour class once or twice a week. This will cost anywhere from $20 to $60 per month. As you progress, you will practice more often. World-class gymnasts usually train six days a week for a total of 25-40 hours. The 1991 world champion, Kim Zmeskal, trains 7 1/2 hours a day! Expenses for gymnastics at Kim's level, including traveling, can cost $10,000 per year.

Events and Equipment

Girls compete in four different events: vaulting, uneven parallel bars, balance beam, and floor exercise. In meets, they must wear a long-sleeve leotard.

Boys have six events: floor exercise, pommel horse, rings, vaulting, parallel bars, and horizontal bar. They must wear a sleeveless jersey, stretch competition pants, and socks. On floor exercise and vaulting, they are allowed to wear shorts and go barefoot.

Competition usually begins when you are 7 years old. At first, you will do simple compulsory routines. Compulsories are exercises that everyone must do. They are designed to teach you all the basic skills. When you become more advanced, you will learn optional routines. Optionals are really fun, because you make them up yourself.

Boys and girls advance at different levels. Boys start in class 7 and work toward class 1. Girls go from level 1 to 10. The Elite level is the highest for boys and girls. Kim Zmeskal, Shannon Miller, and Trent Dimas are Elite gymnasts. They represented the United States in the 1992 Olympics and are training for the 1996 Olympics, too. Other top Americans to watch for are Dominique Dawes and John Roethlisberger. Dominique won the 1994 U.S. championships, and John has won several national titles.

Dominique Dawes,
1994 U.S. champion

9

THE WARM-UP

Gymnastics is a fun sport. Everybody likes to roll and flip, but safety should come first. Always listen to your coach, and be prepared when you go to the gym. Proper practice clothing is very important. If it is cold, a sweat suit is perfect. Socks will keep your feet and ankles warm. If it is not cold, just wear shorts and a T-shirt. Girls can wear a leotard. You need to be able to move freely. Also, never wear jewelry, and keep your hair tied back if it is long.

Getting Your Motor Running

You have to warm up first. There are a few reasons for this. First, stretching all your muscles helps to prevent you from getting hurt. It also makes your body more flexible. All gymnasts need to be extremely flexible. Gymnasts need to be strong, too. Warming up helps to strengthen your muscles.

Your coach will also teach you conditioning exercises, like chin-ups, sit-ups, and push-ups. Most of the time, your conditioning will come at the end of practice.

Nadia Comaneci of Romania won the 1976 Olympics. She also was the first gymnast to score a perfect 10.0. Nadia remembers her early years in gymnastics:

"When you are young, you don't want to warm up," she says. "You just want to jump on the equipment. But you need to warm up first, because you will avoid injuries."

◄ (top) Leg and abdominal exercise
(bottom) Bridge exercise for back and shoulder flexibility

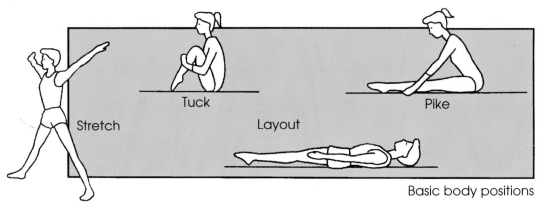

Basic body positions

There are some common warm-up exercises. First, jog around the gym for 5 minutes. This gets your blood moving. It also makes it easier to stretch your muscles.

Next, stand tall with your feet shoulder-width apart. Place your hands on your hips. Now you are going to stretch every part of your body, from head to toe.

To loosen your neck, turn your head from side to side. Pretend you are saying "No" very slowly. Do this about 5 times to each side. Now move your head up and down as if you are saying "Yes" with your head 5 times.

Next, circle your shoulders forward and backward, 5 times each direction. See if you can touch your shoulders to your ears at the top of each circle. Move down to your trunk. With your hands still on your hips, bend from side to side. Now bend forward and backward. To finish, twist your upper body to the left, then to the right.

Take your hands off your hips, and loosen your elbows. Just bend your arms, then straighten them 5 times. Now rotate your wrists in small circles. Finally, wiggle your fingers. Make them look like spiders.

Now you have warmed up everything above the waist. It is time to stretch your legs, ankles, and feet. With your feet together, squat down 5 times to loosen your knees. With your legs straight, rise up on your toes 5 times.

Sit on the ground with your legs apart. Lean forward as far as you can. See if you can touch your chest to the ground. Hold this position for 5 seconds, then repeat 2 more times. This is called a pancake. It is important to stretch slowly. Never bounce or force yourself down. If you do, you might pull a muscle.

Now sit with your legs together and straight. Hold your feet with your hands. Lean forward, and try to place your chest on your knees. Feel your leg muscles stretching. Hold this position for 5 seconds, then repeat 2 more times.

Lie on your back. Bend your legs with your feet flat on the ground. Place your hands flat on the floor by your ears. Now push your stomach toward the ceiling so your back is arched. Hold this position for 5 seconds. This is called a bridge. Try to keep your arms and legs straight. After you come down, round your back, grab your shins, and rock back and forth like a rocking chair.

Bridge
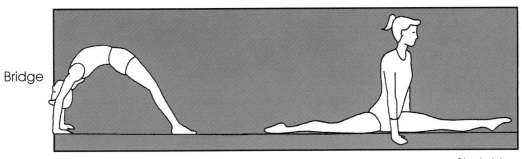
Front split

Stretching

The splits are another stretch. Start by kneeling, then place your left foot straight in front of you. For balance, place your hands on the ground on both sides of your left leg. Now slide your left foot forward as far as possible. Hold this position for 15 seconds. Repeat the same drill with your right leg in front. These are called front splits. The last split is in a straddle position. Stand with your feet as far apart as possible. Slide your feet to the sides, and bend forward at your waist. Place your hands or elbows on the ground for balance. Hold this straddle split for 15 seconds.

Remember to stretch slowly. Never force yourself down so that it hurts. Learning all three splits takes time.

Now you have stretched all your body parts. You are ready to work out!

3

TUMBLING

Tumbling is the first thing beginning gymnasts learn. It is part of the floor exercise, the only event without apparatus. All you need is a mat. Today's floor exercise mats are very springy. Years ago, gymnasts tumbled outdoors on the grass. When gymnastics became an indoor sport in 1948, gymnasts tumbled on the wooden floors you see in a gymnasium. Needless to say, they didn't do the same skills back then that gymnasts do today.

Vitaly Scherbo of Belarus is the 1994 world champion in the men's floor exercise. He excels at this event because he can tumble equally well forward and backward. With practice, so can you.

Forward Roll

The first skill you must learn is a forward roll. Stand up tall with your arms overhead. You should begin all gymnastics skills in this starting position.

To begin a forward roll, squat down like a frog. Place your hands on the mat in front of you. Tuck your chin to your chest, and round your back like a scared cat. Then push off your feet. The back of your head should touch the mat. Now roll like a bowling ball. As you roll, pull your knees tightly toward your chest. This tuck position will roll you back to your feet. As your feet touch the mat, reach forward with your hands. Now stand up tall again.

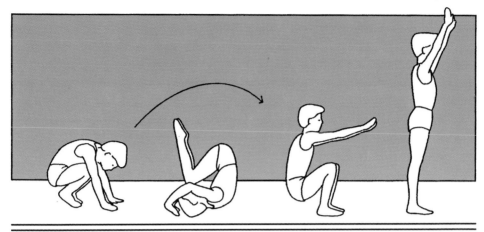

Forward roll

Backward Roll

A backward roll is harder than a forward roll. You might need your coach's help.

Begin in the starting position again. Then squat down. This time, put your hands next to your ears, palms facing the ceiling. Place your chin on your chest, and round your back. Then fall backward. Keep your knees close to your chest. Quickly place your hands on the mat, right next to your ears. Use your hands to push yourself over. As your knees go past your face, push hard with your hands. You will land back on your feet! Stand up tall again. If you get stuck, ask your coach to help you finish the roll.

Headstand

A headstand is a balance skill. Balance skills help you learn to control your body.

First, squat down. Place your hands on the mat in front of you. Next, place your head on the mat about 10 to 12 inches (25 to 30 cm) in front of your hands. Your head and hands should form a triangle.

Headstand

Take your feet off the mat. One at a time, place your knees on your elbows.

Practice this until you can hold it for 5 seconds. If you can, slowly lift your legs off your elbows. Hold your legs together, and stretch them toward the ceiling. This is a headstand. Be sure to keep your body tight. Use your hands for balance.

Handstand

A handstand is similar to a headstand, only it is much harder. But it is one of the most important skills in gymnastics. You will do handstands in every event.

First, get used to supporting your whole body with your arms. Get into the starting position. Step forward with one leg. Now bend over, and place your hands on the mat. Keep your arms straight. Now kick the other leg halfway toward a handstand. Push off the first leg at the same time. For a moment, you will be on your hands. Then step back down, one leg at a time. Practice this drill over and over. When you feel confident, kick a little higher.

Now it is time to go all the way to the handstand. Use a wall to help you keep your balance. Stand a few feet away from the wall. Step forward, and place your hands 6 to 8 inches (15 to 20 cm) from the wall. Kick all the way up to a handstand. Let your feet rest against the wall. Your eyes should stare at your hands the whole time. Practice keeping your body tight. Keep your arms and legs straight, too. Remember to point your toes, just like an All-Star. After awhile, you will not need the wall at all!

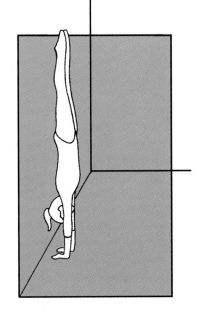

Handstand—using wall for support

BAR SKILLS

This chapter combines two different events that share techniques. Girls compete on the uneven parallel bars. Boys use the horizontal bar, which is also called the high bar. The horizontal bar is one of the oldest events. It is made of steel now, but it used to be wooden. Most likely, it began as a tree limb. The uneven parallel bars are a relatively new event to the sport. The uneven bars and high bar are exciting events to watch because the gymnasts never stop moving.

The basic skills are the same for both the uneven parallel bars and the horizontal bar. In fact, many women do the same tricks on uneven bars that men do on the high bar. A perfect example is American Julianne McNamara. She won a gold medal on uneven bars in the 1984 Olympics. Julianne performed a complicated routine that included skills also seen on the high bar. She made her routine look simple, which is what gymnastics is all about.

"I was pretty confident in my ability," Julianne says, "and by that time, I could hit 10 out of 10 routines in my sleep practically."

Like all successful athletes, Julianne trained very hard. If you want to be an All-Star, you will need lots of practice, too.

At first, you should practice on a bar that is not too high. The low bar of the uneven parallel bars should be perfect for this.

◄ Learning how to do a handstand on bars

Before each turn, rub chalk on the palms of your hands. Chalk absorbs the sweat from your hands. That way you will not slip off the bar.

When you get older, you can wear hand-grips, which are made of leather. Hand-grips help to prevent blisters from forming on your hands. They also give you a better grip on the bar. For now, bare hands are just fine.

Pullover

A pullover is easy if you can do a chin-up. Even if you can't, it is not impossible. Your coach can help you.

Place both hands on top of the bar. Step under the bar with one foot. Then kick the other leg up as hard as you can. Pretend you are kicking a ball toward the ceiling. As you do this, push off the other

Pullover

leg. At the same time, do a chin-up with your arms. Pull the bar toward your stomach. Kick, push, and pull all at once. You will roll around to the top of the bar, resting on your hands and stomach. Now, lift your head up. You are in a front support and ready for the next skill.

Cast

In a front support, your body and arms are straight. When you do a cast, you will bend at the waist. This is also called a pike.

Lean forward with your upper body. Also, pike your legs toward your face. From here, kick your legs backward, but keep them straight. As you kick your legs, push the bar away from your hips. Then come right back to the front support. For a moment, you were only on your hands. This is called a cast. Gymnasts like Shannon Miller can go all the way to a handstand.

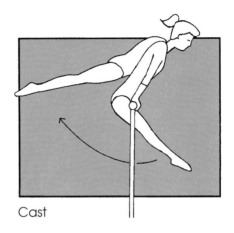
Cast

Back Hip Circle

A back hip circle is two skills in one. It combines a cast and a pullover. Have your coach help you. Start in a front support, then cast your legs away from the bar. As they return to the bar, lean backward. Hold the bar close against your hips. You will swing all the way around the bar. You should finish in another front support. This might make you dizzy at first.

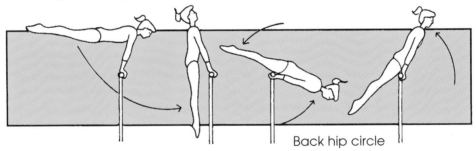
Back hip circle

Basic Swing

Basic swings need a bar that is taller than you are. You can use the boys' horizontal bar. Or you can practice on the high uneven bar.

First, jump up, and grab the bar in an overgrip, with the fingers facing forward. Now you are going to swing back and forth, like a pendulum on a clock. To get started, have your coach push you a little. Each time you swing forward, lift your feet. You will be piked when you do this. At the top of the front swing, straighten your body. Remain straight as you swing to the back. When you get to the back, pike a little bit. Each time you reach the top of the backswing, shift your hands for a better grip. If you forget, you might slip off on the next swing.

As you swing forward again, just relax your body. At the bottom of the swing, you will be arched. Now you are ready to lift your legs again. It is simple once you get the hang of it.

Learning these basic skills is very important. After you master them, you can do just about anything.

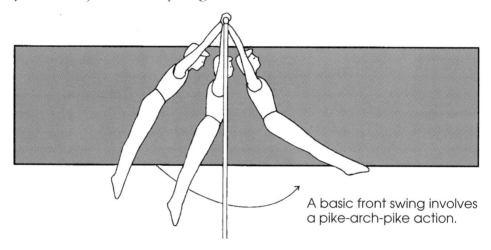

A basic front swing involves a pike-arch-pike action.

THE VALUE OF PRACTICE

American Trent Dimas never dreamed he would win an Olympic medal. "I never thought it was realistic," he says. However, he surprised everyone, including himself. Trent won the gold medal on the horizontal bar at the 1992 Olympics! Before his routine, he was very nervous. Most gymnasts get nervous, and you probably will, too. "There was so much pressure," Trent says. "I really didn't think I was going to be able to compete."

Since Trent had trained like an All-Star, he did the best routine of his life. If you practice hard, you might find yourself in the same situation one day.

VAULTING

Like tumbling, vaulting is for both boys and girls. It requires a springboard and a horse.

Vaulting is a very old event. Ancient frescos have been discovered on the island of Crete that show a man jumping over a live bull. Centuries later, gymnasts jumped over wooden boxes. Then the vaulting horse was developed, and it actually resembled a real horse. It had a neck on one end and a tail on the other!

Today the vaulting horse looks the same on both ends. It also has springs inside and is padded on top. Good vaulters have strong legs, which enable them to jump high.

American Mary Lou Retton was one of the best vaulters in her day. She used her incredible vaulting ability in the 1984 Olympics. Vaulting was her last event in the all-around competition. She needed to score a perfect 10.0 to win the gold. Mary Lou performed a beautiful vault and "stuck" the landing. That means she landed without taking any extra steps. She scored a 10.0 and became the Olympic all-around champion!

Before you learn to vault like Mary Lou, you need to learn the basics. The first step is learning how to use the springboard.

Jumping onto the springboard

The Approach

The approach begins with the run. Practice jumping onto the springboard. For now, do not even use the vaulting horse. Place the springboard in front of a big soft mat. Jump off the springboard onto the mat.

Begin about 30 to 40 feet (9 to 12 m) away from the springboard. Run toward the springboard, but not too fast. As you near the springboard, jump off one foot. You will land with both feet right on the springboard. As you do, push off with your feet by straightening your legs. Try to push the springboard through the floor! As you do this, lift your arms upward. Jump forward onto the soft mat. Practice this until you can jump really high!

Squat-On

Now you are ready to use the horse, but you will not go over at first. Your coach will help you learn a squat-on. It is easy.

Begin your approach, then jump onto the springboard. After you hit the springboard, reach for the horse. Place your hands right on top of it. Then squat your knees up to your chest. Place your feet on the horse, between your hands. Then stop. Now stand up, and jump forward onto the landing mat.

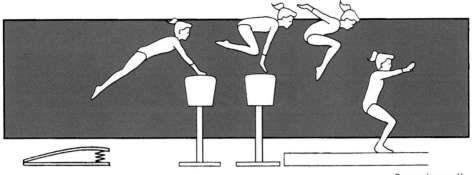

Squat vault

Squat Vault

A squat vault is just like a squat-on, but your feet never touch the horse. Only your hands do. With your coach spotting, use the same approach as before. Hit the springboard, and reach for the horse. When your hands touch the horse, push hard. Pull your knees up and through your arms. Your feet will go over the horse completely. Lift your chest, and land on your feet.

When your feet land, be sure to bend your knees. Also, hold your arms in front of you. This will help you "stick" the landing, just like Mary Lou did!

Coming off the horse in pike position

25

BALANCE BEAM

The balance beam is considered to be the most difficult event for girls. It takes a great deal of concentration because the balance beam is only 4 inches (10 cm) wide!

The balance beam has gone through many changes. It used to be a long tree limb supported a few feet off the ground. Other early beams were nothing more than a pair of two-by-fours nailed together.

Like other gymnastics equipment, the design of the balance beam has improved tremendously. Thirty years ago, the beam was constructed only of wood. Now it is padded on top and covered with a nonslip surface.

American Shannon Miller is exceptional on the balance beam. She rarely loses her balance. As a result, she won the gold medal on the balance beam at the 1994 world championships. She even has a skill named after her called the "Miller." It looks fairly risky, because she dives backward and stops in a handstand. Of her world title, Shannon says, "I thought it was one of my best beam routines." But being the perfectionist she is, Shannon adds, "I probably could have held my "Miller" longer than I did."

◄ Shannon Miller (USA), 1992 Olympic all-around silver medalist, 1993 and 1994 world all-around champion, 1994 balance beam world champion

Before you attempt to reach Shannon's skill level, you should practice on a floor beam. It is only a few inches off the floor. That way you don't have far to fall, and you will probably fall a lot at first.

Walking across the balance beam

Walking

Your first challenge is to walk across the beam. With good posture, stand at one end of the beam. Hold your chin up, and relax your shoulders. Focus your eyes on the other end of the beam. For balance, hold your arms out to the side, like a tightrope walker. Now you are ready to walk.

Take small steps at first, and stay on the balls of your feet. If you lose your balance, stop. Use your arms to avoid falling, and bend your knees a little. It is important to learn how to stay on the beam.

Half Turn

Once you are comfortable walking, it is time to turn around. Stand with one foot slightly in front of the other. Then rise onto the balls of your feet. This makes turning much easier. Lift your arms over your head. Now you are prepared to do a half turn.

If your right foot is in front, turn to the left. If your left foot is in front, turn to the right. Start turning by looking for the other end of the beam. As your head turns, quickly turn your body, too. Remember to stay on the balls of your feet.

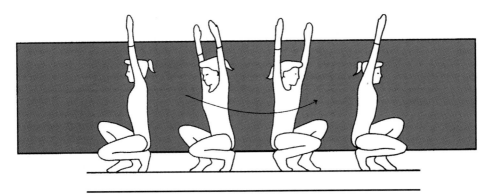

Squat turn

Squat Turn

To do a squat turn, begin with one foot slightly in front of the other. Keep your head up and your back flat. If you slouch, you might fall. Hold your arms overhead. Just like before, turn your head, then turn your body.

Dismounts

After you feel comfortable on the floor beam, move up to the high beam. Try not to think of the high beam as being scary. It is still 4 inches (10 cm) wide, just like the floor beam. Try to stay calm so you can concentrate. If your legs are shaking, you need to practice on the floor beam longer. If you feel confident, you are ready for a simple dismount.

Stand at the end of the beam, facing out. Lift your arms, and jump onto the landing mat below. Remember to bend your knees when you land. This is called a stretch jump.

Now add a tuck to the stretch jump. Stand at the end of the beam again. Then jump off, and tuck your knees briefly toward your chest. Extend your legs again for the landing. This is called a tuck jump. Now that you have learned the basics, you are ready to try more advanced elements.

POMMEL HORSE

The pommel horse is an extremely demanding boys' event. One slip of the hand, and you can fall. Like the vaulting horse, the pommel horse once looked like a real horse. Now it is completely flat on top. The two handles on top are called pommels. In the 1800s, gymnasts supported themselves on the pommels in various positions. Today, gymnasts perform intricate swinging combinations on and around the pommels. The pommel horse requires strong arms and shoulders, because you are always on your hands.

American Mark Sohn is an expert on the pommel horse. He performs skills that have never been done before. From 1989 to 1991, Mark won four consecutive national collegiate pommel horse titles while at Penn State University. Then he decided to compete internationally. In the 1994 world championships, he had the highest pommel horse score in the preliminaries. That meant he qualified for the finals. If he scored the highest again, he would become the pommel horse world champion.

When it was Mark's turn to perform in the finals, disaster struck. His legs separated briefly on his first skill. That small mistake cost him a tenth of a point from the judges. The winning score was 9.712, and Mark scored 9.625. He placed sixth. One tenth more, and he

◄ Mark Sohn (USA), four time NCAA champion on pommel horse and a finalist in the 1992 and 1994 world championships

would have been world champion! After the competition, Mark reflected on his disappointment. "It was mine to win, seemed like," Mark says. "....But the fact that I was in first [after preliminaries] makes it a lot easier to swallow the whole situation."

Even though Mark didn't win a medal, he displayed the sportsmanship of an All-Star. He accepted his defeat with grace. You may experience similar situations in gymnastics, especially on a difficult event like the pommel horse. In order to perform like Mark Sohn, you will need to learn the fundamentals. The following is a brief introduction to the difficult pommel horse event.

Support Travels

Grab the pommels with both hands, and jump so that you are supporting your body with your hands and arms. Your hands should be in the middle of the pommels, or slightly forward. Travel sideways to the end without falling. First, go to the right. Lean forward toward your right hand. Then quickly move your left hand over in front of your right. Both hands will be on the same pommel. Then move to the end of the horse. Be sure to keep your arms straight. You have just performed a downhill support travel. You moved from the pommels down to the end of the horse.

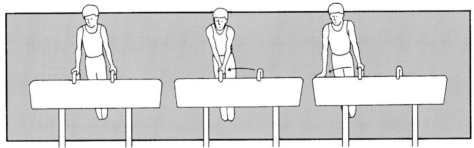

Support travel

Next is an uphill support travel, which is a little harder. Start on the left end of the horse. Put your left hand on the end. Put your right hand on the left pommel. Now push off your left hand and lean to the right. Your left hand reaches in front of your right on the pommel. Then switch your right hand to the right pommel. See if you can combine an uphill and downhill travel!

Pendulum Swing

To swing, begin in a support, both hands on the pommels. Now swing your legs from side to side. Straddle your legs at the top of each swing. Your shoulders should move opposite to your legs. When your legs go left, your shoulders go right. Remember to keep your legs straight all the time, and point your toes. This makes the swing easier, and it looks better, too!

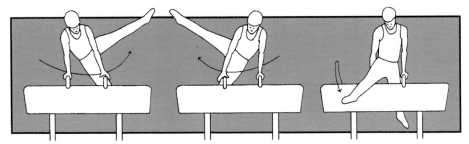

Pendulum swing and forward leg cut

Leg Cuts

After your swing is smooth, it is time for leg cuts. You will learn forward leg cuts and backward leg cuts. Start your pendulum swing, back and forth. Then release your left hand. As you do, quickly swing your left leg to the front. Be sure to grab the pommel with your left hand again. Never sit on the horse. After the leg cut, you will be straddling the horse. This is called a forward leg cut.

Now try a backward leg cut. Just swing your left leg from the front to the back. Remember to release the pommel with your left hand. Also, shift your weight to your right hand. Now try the same thing with the right leg. Swing your right leg to the front. Then swing it from the front to the back. Let go of the pommel with your right hand. Practice this drill over and over.

RINGS

The ring event began in Italy. The event itself used to be called the flying rings. Men and women performed on a pair of rings that swung back and forth. The rings were made of iron and covered with leather. Now the event is for men only, and the rings must hang as still as possible. Modern rings are constructed of wood or fiberglass, which makes them much lighter than before.

The best gymnasts on rings are usually very strong. The event requires swinging skills and feats of sheer strength. An iron cross is an example of a strength skill. The 1993 and 1994 world champion on rings is Yuri Chechi from Italy. Yuri combines his strength and swing elements like no other gymnast. He always seems to be in complete control of the rings. With years of practice, you can master this event, too.

Rings is another event where you need to use chalk. When you start to learn harder skills, you will wear hand-grips. For now, bare hands are okay.

Inverted Hang

The first skill is a simple hang, only you will be upside-down. When your coach lifts you to the rings, be sure to get a good grip. Then

◄ Yuri Chechi (Italy), the world champion on rings, 1993 and 1994

tuck your legs up between the rings. When you are upside down, straighten your legs and your hips. Your arms and body should be completely straight. If you shake at first, that's normal. Just tighten the muscles in your stomach. Practice holding this inverted hang until you are completely still.

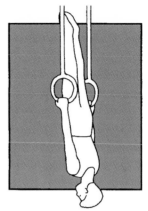

Inverted hang

Piked Inverted Hang

From the straight inverted hang, you are ready for the next position. All you have to do is pike your hips. Bring your knees to your nose. The closer the better. This is called a piked inverted hang.

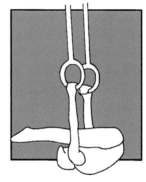

Piked inverted hang

Skin-the-Cat

Now that you are doing a piked inverted hang, try a skin-the-cat. That is where you let your body roll down backward slowly. Your arms will be behind you. Your toes will point toward the floor. Allow your body to relax completely. Feel the stretch in your shoulders. Have your coach spot you.

From this position, pull your body back up. Pass through a piked inverted hang first, then a straight inverted hang. Pull hard!

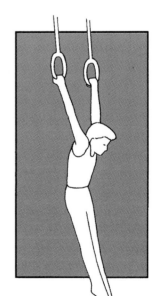

Skin-the-cat

Basic Swing

The first three skills have been static elements. In other words, your body is still. Now it is time to develop a basic swing. A good solid swing will help you to learn more advanced skills.

Begin in a hanging position. Keep your body tight and your legs together. When you start to swing, you need to stay in control. If your body gets too loose, you will go crooked.

Begin swinging very low by lifting your feet forward. Then let them swing backward naturally. When your feet swing forward, allow your chest to hollow. When your feet swing backward, arch your back a little.

When you swing, your hands have a job to do, too. As your feet swing forward, your hands should turn in. That means your thumbs are to the rear. Also, you should pull the rings out to the sides a bit. When your feet swing to the back, your hands should turn out with thumbs to the front. Also, push the rings out to the sides slightly.

Practice swinging over and over but not too high at first. If your basic swing is good, it will feel smooth. If it is jerky at all, work on it some more.

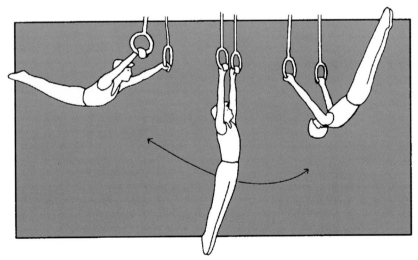

Basic swing: Heels lift at back, feet lift at front

PARALLEL BARS

The parallel bars have remained pretty much the same throughout history. Originally, the two bars were wooden, but most of today's bars are made of fiberglass. The exercises performed on this men's event consist mainly of swinging skills.

You need strong arms to do well on parallel bars. This event has always been American Bart Conner's favorite. Bart won the gold medal on parallel bars in the 1984 Olympics. He had worked very hard on that event all his life. He even remembers the first time he saw a set of parallel bars. At age 10, Bart could already do a handstand. "I could walk all around the house on my hands," Bart remembers.

Because of his talent, Bart was invited to watch the local high school gymnastics team one day. The coach put Bart on the parallel bars, and he felt right at home. "I just swung back and forth a couple of times and went right to a handstand," Bart says. "It was my first time on the parallel bars."

Ever since, Bart has always loved the parallel bars. "These initial experiences when you are young pave the way for a lot of things," Bart says. "Because I had success at the beginning, I had confidence."

◄ Bart Conner (USA) won the gold medal on parallel bars at the 1984 Olympics.

You may not be able to swing to a handstand at first. However, you can still build the confidence that Bart talks about. Like all gymnastics events, you need to start at the beginning. Be sure to master each skill before moving on to the next one.

There are a few different styles of swinging on parallel bars. Before you start, you need to adjust the height and width of the bars. Ask your coach to show you how. Most people measure the width with their forearm. From your elbow to your fingertips is a good width. The bars should be high enough so your feet will not hit the floor. Your coach will help you with the height, too. Remember to tighten the bars after you adjust them.

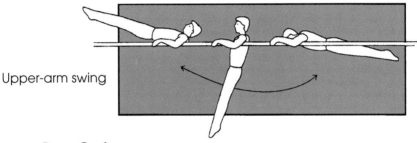

Upper-arm swing

Upper-Arm Swing

After you chalk up, walk to the middle of the bars. Then jump up, and support yourself on your upper arms. Your elbows will be bent, and your hands will grip the bars in front of you. Now you can start swinging back and forth. Just lift your feet in front, then let them swing to the back. This may feel uncomfortable on your arms at first, but that is normal. Some gymnasts wear long-sleeve sweatshirts when they practice on parallel bars. This helps to protect their arms.

The goal of any swing is to keep your body straight. When you lift your feet forward, try not to pike too much. When your feet swing behind you, try not to arch too much either.

Back Uprise

After you learn the upper-arm swing, you are ready for a back uprise. When your feet swing behind you, push yourself into a straight-arm support. You will need a high back swing to do this. If you cannot make it all the way up, ask your coach for help.

Support Swing

After the back uprise, you will be in a straight-arm support. That means only your hands are on the bars. It is time to work on a support swing. This is the swing you see most often when you watch the Olympics. You can do all kinds of tricks from this swing.

Before you start, remember to keep your arms and body straight. Also, swing low at first. If your arms start to shake, you are going too high.

Now, lift your feet forward a little. Also, push your chest forward with your arms. Your body will start to swing back and forth like a pendulum. For balance, keep your shoulders directly over your hands. Eventually, you will be able to swing up to a handstand, just like Bart Conner did. For now, it is best to swing low and develop your confidence.

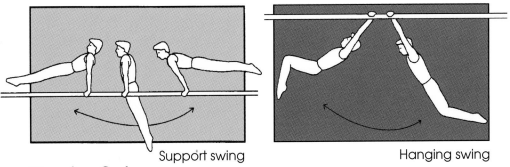

Support swing   Hanging swing

Hanging Swing

This last swing is done below the bars in a hang. It is just like the basic swing on the horizontal bar, only here, you are allowed to bend your knees so your feet do not hit the ground.

Grab the bars with your fingers facing outward. Place your thumbs on top of the bars, too. Start your swing by lifting your knees in front of you. Pull down with the arms a little. Practice this swing until you can feel the rhythm.

It is important to take your time when learning these swings. Never swing so high that it scares you. Remember what Bart Conner said. Your early experiences on any event can affect you throughout your career. So try to make them positive and enjoyable.

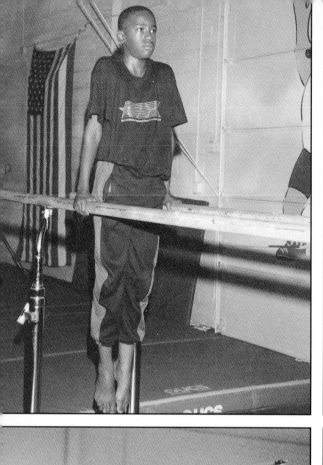

THE CHALLENGES AHEAD

What Does It Take?

Now you know about the different gymnastics events. However, there is much more to this wonderful sport. Gymnastics is both an individual and a team sport. At the Olympics, for example, the first competition determines the team champion. After that, the individual all-around champion is crowned. Finally, the best gymnasts in each event are decided in the apparatus finals.

Bart Conner won the gold on parallel bars in the 1984 Olympics. He also won the gold with his five teammates. Bart says the team victory meant much more to him. "Even though I did win an individual medal," Bart says, "it had nowhere near the impact on me emotionally as did the team medal."

In the past, there were six gymnasts on the Olympic team. In 1996, however, seven gymnasts will make the team.

To compete in the Olympics, you must turn at least 15 years old during the Olympic year. Beginning in 1997, the minimum age will be 16.

This age requirement usually has no effect on male gymnasts. Men reach their prime between the ages of 18 and 25. That is when they develop most of their body strength.

◀ (upper left) Parallel bar mount
(upper right) Floor exercise cat leap
(lower left) Learning a forward roll on the beam
(lower right) Practicing a leap on the beam

AMERICAN SUCCESS

Gymnastics used to be dominated by the Russians and Japanese. But in 1984, the United States finally broke through to the top. At the Los Angeles Olympics, the U.S. men's team won the gold medal. The inspired Americans defeated a powerful Chinese team, which had just won the 1983 world championships.

Individually, Peter Vidmar placed second all-around for the United States. The all-around is determined by totaling a competitor's scores from every event. He also won a gold medal on pommel horse. Peter says he was very happy to win the gold for his coach. His teammate Bart Conner became Olympic champion on parallel bars. Bart was competing in his third Olympics!

Also in 1984, Mary Lou Retton became the first and only American woman to win the Olympic all-around. She needed to score a perfect 10.0 on her last event, the vault. And she made it!

After 1984, American gymnasts won only a few medals in world championships or Olympics. But that trend changed in 1991. Kim Zmeskal became the first American all-around world champion.

Unfortunately, Kim didn't win any individual medals in the 1992 Olympics. But Trent Dimas did. He won the gold medal on horizontal bar, the first Olympic gold for an American man since 1984.

If you watched the 1992 Olympics, you may remember that Shannon Miller placed second all-around. Tatiana Gutsu of the former Soviet Union won by .012, a very close margin. However, Shannon won a total of five medals at those Olympics.

Despite the overall loss to Tatiana Gutsu, Shannon kept working hard after that. In 1993 she became the all-around world champion. Then, in 1994, she won the world championships again. She's the only American gymnast ever to win two consecutive world championships. Shannon is a true All-Star!

World-class female gymnasts are much younger. Tatiana Gutsu of Ukraine was just 15 when she won the 1992 Olympics. However, there are exceptions. American Kathy Johnson competed in the 1984 Olympics when she was 24!

Age is not important as long as you are healthy and enjoy the sport. Bart Conner competed in three Olympics. He retired from competition when he was 26.

"I think the most important quality you need is desire," Bart says. "It's nice to have the physical attributes of being quick, strong, light, and flexible. But most of those things can be developed if you have the desire."

The 1976 Olympic champion, Nadia Comaneci, agrees. "A lot of kids are born with strength, and some are flexible," she says. "Even if you aren't born with a strong body, you can become strong."

Nadia also says a young gymnast should never give up. "Try a little harder every day," she says. "Feel as though you accomplished something, no matter how little it is."

Gymnastics is more than just a sport. It is a worthwhile challenge that provides you with many things. Physically, your body will become very strong and flexible. You will also develop self-discipline, confidence, and integrity as an individual. As a member of a team, you will learn cooperation and establish many friendships. With qualities like those, you can hardly go wrong.

Gymnasts applying resin to hands as they get ready to practice

GLOSSARY

All-around: The total score from all four events for women, or all six events for men

Apparatus: Gymnastics equipment

Back hip circle: A skill in which you spin backward around a bar, holding the bar against your hips

Back uprise: A skill on parallel bars in which you swing from an upper-arm position to a straight-arm support position during the backswing

Balance beam: A women's event; a bar of wood measuring 4 inches (10 cm) wide, 16 feet (5 m) long, and 4 feet (1 m) high

Basic: A fundamental skill

Bridge: A position in which you arch your back and support yourself with your hands and feet; Also called a back bend

Cast: To swing your legs away from the bar during a front support

Chalk: Dry, white powder you rub on your hands to keep from slipping from the apparatus

Chin-up: An exercise in which you pull your chin up to the bar

Compulsory: A routine, or exercise, that all gymnasts must do

Dismount: The final skill in a routine. It begins on the apparatus and finishes on the floor.

Downhill support travel: A basic drill on the pommel horse in which you move on your hands sideways from the pommels to the end of the horse

Elite: The highest competitive level for a gymnast

Floor exercise: A tumbling event for men and women performed on a mat that measures 40 feet by 40 feet (12 m by 12 m)

Half turn: A basic skill involving a 180-degree change in direction

Hand-grips: Leather guards that protect the palms of the hand and provide a better grip

Handstand: A skill in which you balance upside down on your hands

Hanging swing: To swing with your entire body below the parallel bar

Headstand: A skill in which you balance upside down on your head and hands

Horizontal bar: A men's event that features nonstop circular swings and high-flying release-regrasp skills

Horse: A piece of equipment used for vaulting and pommel horse that measures about 63 inches (160 cm) long by 14 inches (36 cm) wide

Inverted: Upside down

Inverted hang: A skill on rings in which you hang upside down

Iron cross: A strength skill on rings in which the arms are held straight out to the sides

Layout: Straight body position

Leg cut: A skill in which one leg swings from one side of the pommel horse to the other

Mount: The first skill in a routine. It begins on the floor and finishes on the apparatus.

Optional: A routine composed by the gymnast

Overgrip: Hand position on a single bar, with fingers facing forward

Pancake: A position in which the legs are straddled and the chest is touching the floor

Parallel bars: A men's event consisting of two parallel bars measuring about 11 feet, 5 inches (3.5 m) in length. The width of the bars is adjustable.

Pendulum swing: Back-and-forth motion of most simple swings

Pike: When the body is bent at the hips only

Piked inverted hang: A skill on rings in which you hang upside down and bend at the hips

Pommel: One of two handles on the pommel horse

Pommel horse: A men's event involving circular and pendular swings while in a straight-arm support

Rings: A men's event involving swinging and held strength skills

Routine: A series of skills that a gymnast performs in competition

Skin-the-cat: A hanging position on rings in which the arms are behind the body

Split: A position in which the legs are spread apart 180 degrees.

Spot: To assist a gymnast or to prevent him or her from falling

Springboard: Equipment used to jump over the vaulting horse

Squat: Position in which the legs and hips are bent

Squat-on: Vaulting skill in which you land on the horse in a squat position

Squat turn: Balance beam skill in which you turn around in a squat position

Squat vault: Vaulting skill in which the legs bend and pass through the arms and over the horse

Stick: To land a dismount without moving or taking extra steps

Straddle: When the legs are far apart to the sides, but not completely in a split

Straight-arm support: Any position in which the body is supported by the arms

Support swing: To swing on parallel bars in a straight-arm support

Support travel: To move from one part of the pommel horse to another while in a straight-arm support

Tuck: To bend the body at the knees and hips. The tuck is similar to the squat.

Tuck jump: To jump in the air and bend the knees and hips

Tumbling: Skills performed in floor exercise

Undergrip: Hand position on a single bar, with the fingers facing toward you

Uneven parallel bars: A women's event consisting of two parallel bars. One bar is higher than the other, and the width is adjustable.

Uphill support travel: To move from the end of the pommel horse to the middle while in a straight-arm support

Upper-arm swing: To swing on the parallel bars while in an upper-arm support

Vaulting: An event for men and women that requires a springboard and a vaulting horse

Vaulting horse: Apparatus used for vaulting

FURTHER READING

Duden, Jane. *Men's & Women's Gymnastics.* MacMillan, 1992

Haycock, Kate. *Gymnastics.* MacMillan, 1991

Kuklin, Susan. *Going to My Gymnastics Class.* MacMillan, 1991

United States Gymnastics Federation Staff. *I Can Do Gymnastics: Essential Skills for Beginning Gymnasts.* Masters Press, 1993

YMCA Staff. *YMCA Gymnastics.* Human Kinetics, 1991

INDEX